WELCOME TO

Collect the special coins in this book. You will earn one gold coin for every chapter you read.

Once you have finished all the chapters, find out what to do with your gold coins at the back of the book.

With special thanks to Conrad Mason

For Adam Bampfylde

www.beastquest.co.uk

ORCHARD BOOKS

First published in Great Britain in 2018 by The Watts Publishing Group

1 3 5 7 9 10 8 6 4 2

Text © 2018 Beast Quest Limited
Cover and inside illustrations by Steve Sims
© Beast Quest Limited 2018

Beast Quest is a registered trademark of Beast Quest Limited
Series created by Beast Quest Limited, London

A CIP catalogue record for this book is available from the British Library.

ISBN 978 1 40834 329 6

Printed in Great Britain

The paper and board used in this book are made from wood from responsible sources

Orchard Books
An imprint of Hachette Children's Group
Part of The Watts Publishing Group Limited
Carmelite House, 50 Victoria Embankment, London EC4Y 0DZ

An Hachette UK Company
www.hachette.co.uk
www.hachettechildrens.co.uk

Skra R
The Night Scavenger

by Adam Blade

ORCHARD

MAP OF AVANTIA

THE PIT OF FIRE

STONEWIN VOLCANO

KING HUGO'S PALACE

THE CITY

ERRINEL

THE JUNGLE VILLAGE

THE DARK WOOD

CONTENTS

I'd forgotten how much I hate this kingdom. The fields full of crops. The clear blue skies. The simple, smiling people, going about their petty lives.

Well, all that is about to change. When I get my hands on the Book of Derthsin, *I will have a whole new world of evil magic at my fingertips.*

King Hugo will pay for his smugness. Avantia will tremble. Its protector Beasts will suffer. But above all, it is Tom who will feel my wrath.

And as he perishes, it will be my smiling face he sees.

It's good to be back!

Malvel

SHADOW PATH

"What in all Avantia is it?" asked Elenna. She gazed upwards, shielding her eyes.

Tom shook his head. "I don't know, but I don't like it."

Looming over them was a vast golden column, as thick as a tree trunk, with smooth, rounded sides that gleamed softly. It was the only sight to be seen in the lonely countryside that stretched out around them; there wasn't even a signpost to mark the border between

the Kingdoms of Avantia and Rion. A chill wind blew, and Tom felt a shiver run down his spine.

From the top of the column, a sculpted golden face glared down at them, frozen in a savage snarl. The face of Grymon the Biting Horror. Just a few moments ago, Tom and Elenna had defeated the Beast, and it had transformed into this strange golden edifice.

It feels wrong, somehow, thought Tom. *Almost as though it's...evil. And no wonder!* Grymon had been no ordinary Beast. Tom's oldest enemy, the sorcerer Malvel, had summoned the creature from the depths of the Netherworld using an ancient spell book – the *Book of Derthsin.*

And if we don't get the book back soon, there's no telling what other horrors Malvel will conjure to lay waste to Avantia.

"If only we had some sort of clue," Tom murmured. "Something to tell us where Malvel might now be headed..."

Elenna frowned. "Maybe we do," she said. Her gaze travelled down the length of the column, then she pointed at something on the ground. "What do you see there?"

Tom stared at the foot of the golden structure, then gave up. "Nothing," he admitted. "Just rocks and grass. And the shadow of the column."

"Exactly!" said Elenna, grinning. "A shadow… But look, see where the sun is."

Tom glanced up, and saw that the sky was clouded over with a pale haze. Then it hit him. "A shadow with no sunshine! That's not normal, that's—"

"Magic!" Elenna interrupted. "I say we follow the path of the shadow."

Tom nodded. "It's the best lead we've got."

As they turned away from the column, heading back to where Tom's horse Storm was patiently waiting, a ghostly figure swam up out of the ground. It was a young man in blue robes, with the tall, pointed hat of a wizard. *Daltec!*

"What a relief to see you both safe and sound!" said Daltec.

"How is Aduro?" asked Elenna.

A cloud passed across Daltec's face. "See for yourselves." He stepped to one side and behind him appeared some sort of laboratory, the tables cluttered with books and vials of bubbling chemicals. The wizard Aduro lay on a bed in the midst of it all, his eyes closed, his face almost as white as his long hair and beard. Tom's heart sank at the sight of his old friend looking so weak.

"I'm still searching for a cure," said Daltec. "But Malvel's magic is strong.

Whatever sleep he has put Aduro into is both deep and terrible..." He shook his head and smiled. "On the other hand, I have some assistance."

A girl stepped into view, perhaps five years older than Tom and Elenna. She had short black hair and was dressed in a red robe like Daltec's blue one. As she smiled at them, Tom caught a glimpse of something moving gently at her back – a pair of delicate wings like those of a butterfly.

"You must be from Henkrall!" said Tom.

"That's right!" said the girl. "The Circle of Wizards has members from every kingdom. I am to be the new

witch of Henkrall, the first since the fall of the tyrant, Kensa." She gave Daltec a playful nudge. "Well? Aren't you going to introduce me?"

"Lyra, this is Tom and Elenna," said Daltec. "Tom and Elenna, meet Lyra. She's been so helpful. More helpful than I could have imagined, really..." He tailed off, gazing at Lyra with big, wide eyes.

Elenna laughed. "Daltec, are you blushing?"

The young wizard turned even redder. "I...er... Of course not! Wizards don't blush!"

Tom grinned. "Well, I hope together you can find a cure." Then he sighed as he remembered the Quest which lay ahead. "I wish Elenna and I had wings like you, Lyra. It would certainly help us catch Malvel, wherever he is."

Lyra's brow creased in thought. "It's not a bad idea, actually."

"You mean you can give them wings?" asked Daltec, in awe.

Lyra laughed. "If only! My powers aren't that strong yet. But that horse..." She pointed at Storm, who was quietly grazing by a pile of boulders. Closing her eyes, she put her fingers to her temple, muttering something under her breath.

Storm reared up and let out a whinny, as though a bee had stung him. Then two feathered black wings sprouted from his flanks, spreading out like those of a giant raven.

"Wow!" gasped Elenna.

Tom felt a smile spread across his

face. "That's amazing, Lyra! This will make our Quest ten times easier. Come on, Elenna!"

He sprinted to Storm and vaulted into the saddle, then bent down to give Elenna a hand so she could clamber up behind him. Storm whinnied again, prancing across the grass and flexing his new wings with pride.

"Remarkable," said Daltec. "But I feel the vision fading. Good luck, friends!"

"And be careful," added Lyra, as the image began to melt away. "My spell won't last for ever..."

"Oh, one last thing!" said Daltec. "Good news – Queen Aroha has given birth to a baby boy! King Hugo is with her, but he will soon return to Avantia, now that Malvel threatens our kingdom again."

"Is that wise?" asked Tom. "Surely

he should stay safe in Tangala, out of harm's way?"

But Daltec and Lyra were already gone, disappeared into thin air.

"It's just us now," said Elenna. "Time to face Malvel again. Are you ready?"

Tom nodded and stroked Storm's neck. At once, the stallion leapt up high, and Tom felt himself jolted backwards as they took flight, jerking upwards with every beat of the giant black wings. As the wind blew through his hair, he felt Elenna's arms tight round his waist, and his heart filled with courage.

While there's blood in my veins, I'll always be ready!

A TERRIBLE DISCOVERY

The ground seemed to shrink as
Storm flew higher into the clouded
sky. But as Tom peered down, he
could still see the thin dark line
of the magical shadow spreading
out from the base of the golden
column. It ran west over the desolate
countryside, and Tom flicked the

reins, steering Storm to fly in its path. They followed the shadow, with no sound but the roaring of the wind and Storm's heavy wingbeats.

Once again Tom felt a creeping sensation run through him. *That golden column – what does it mean?* Perhaps he would find the answer in the *Book of Derthsin*, if they managed to recover it.

"Look!" said Elenna, pointing ahead. "It's the Northern Mountains."

Sure enough, a collection of stark grey peaks pierced the clouds on the horizon.

"Do you think Malvel came this way?" Elenna wondered out loud.

"I hope so," said Tom. *But if he*

did, what terrible new Beast is
he planning to summon from the
Netherworld?

Storm neighed and swooped down low, gliding on a thermal. "I think he's enjoying having wings," said Elenna, with a grin.

"I don't blame him!" laughed Tom.

They flew lower, skimming over a patch of woodland. Storm's hooves flicked at the leaves of the highest treetops, then they flew out over a field beyond. Tom narrowed his eyes as he saw a village at the bottom of the field. But half the buildings were destroyed, with roofs caved in and walls crumbled into rubble that lay across the streets. "What happened here?" he wondered out loud.

"I can see villagers," said Elenna. "They're all gathered around that one big ruined building..."

Tom hesitated. *Every moment we waste, Malvel will be getting*

further away! But he couldn't ignore whatever danger these people were in.

"We'd better investigate," said Tom, steering his stallion lower.

Storm angled his wings and they

flew over the rooftops. Tom saw that the villagers were panicking, shouting to each other and pointing at something poking out from beneath the rubble of the big building. He drew in a sharp breath – it was a man's hand, scrabbling for something to grab hold of.

"I think he's stuck under there!" gasped Elenna.

Tom peered closer and saw that a heavy wooden beam lay across where the man's body was buried. *We've got to lift it off!* He flicked the reins, bringing Storm down to land beside the rubble. The villagers backed away, startled by the sight of the winged horse.

"Friends!" Tom called to them. "Do you have any rope? Tie it to the beam, and we'll take the other end."

As Tom and Elenna dismounted, the closest villagers held a short whispered conversation. Then one of them hurried to a nearby stable and brought out a coil of thick rope. A few moments later, they had one end tied around the massive beam, and passed the other end to Elenna.

Elenna fastened the rope tightly to Storm's saddle, then Tom patted Storm on his rump. "Now, boy... Pull!"

Letting out a huge neigh, Storm beat his wings and surged up into the sky.

Creeeak! The beam groaned as the

rope snapped taut.

"You can do it, Storm!" shouted
Elenna.

Tom's horse struggled, flapping desperately. But inch by inch, the beam began to give. Finally, with a great clattering sound, it scraped free and went tumbling down the heap of rubble to the ground.

As Storm circled round to land at Tom's side, the trapped man pulled himself free, coughing and spluttering. He was big and broad-shouldered, with a thick brown beard.

"I know him!" whispered Elenna, as the man staggered to the ground, wiping brick dust from his face. "It's Ched, remember? We met him on our Quest to save Raffkor."

"Of course!" said Tom. "But it

looks like he's hurt."

Ched was stumbling, clutching at one leg. His trousers were stained red with blood.

"The beam must have broken his leg," said Tom. He reached for his belt, taking out his green jewel and holding it over Ched's injured limb. The gem glimmered with magic, and there was a cracking sound as the bones slid back into place.

"Aargh!" cried Ched. "Who did that?" Then his gaze fell on Tom, and his eyebrows shot up. "Am I seeing things? Is that Tom? The Master of the Beasts?"

"Master of the Beasts?" scoffed a tall woman with plaited red hair.

"Some Master! Where was he when the earthquake struck?"

"There was an earthquake here?" asked Elenna.

"What else do you think caused this?" snapped an old man, flinging his arm out to indicate the wreckage all around. "And Arcta the Mountain Giant didn't come to help us, like he has before. Our homes are ruined and it will take seasons to rebuild without the mountain giant's help."

Worry stirred in Tom's gut. He took his shield from his back. Every one of the Beast tokens had turned ghostly pale, drained of their power by a bolt of magical lightning from Malvel's staff. The same spell had put Epos into an enchanted sleep, and Tom wondered if the Dark Magic had spread from the tokens to the other Good Beasts. *I hope they're not hurt.*

A hostile voice shouted: "Explain yourself, Master of the Beasts!"

Tom looked around and saw that the villagers were closing in on him and Elenna, glaring fiercely. He put away his shield and held out his hands. "I promise, I'll find out what's going on."

He turned to Elenna. "The shadow path leads towards Arcta's domain. We can search for him as we follow it." Elenna nodded and Tom turned and pushed through the crowd,

making for where Storm waited
patiently with folded wings.

"He's abandoning us!" screeched
an angry villager.

"I'll find Arcta – you have my
word," said Tom. Then he and Elenna
clambered up into Storm's saddle.
As Storm took off again, Tom did his
best to ignore the angry shouts of
the villagers which followed them.

Storm circled once above the
village, then Tom flicked the reins,
steering his stallion towards the
Northern Mountains again. Rising
above them all was a tall, jagged
mountain wreathed in mist, which
Tom recognised at once. "That way!"
he told Storm. "That's where Arcta

lives." The horse darted forward, swooping up the mountainside towards the summit.

"Look!" yelled Elenna suddenly,

gripping Tom's waist hard.

Tom saw vultures circling over a patch of woodland on the mountainside. And below, lying across the crushed trunks of several trees, was a massive brown-furred figure. He was sprawled with limbs askew, as though he had fallen from a great height, and he was utterly still. Tom felt a lump forming in his throat.

Is Arcta dead?

THE NIGHT SCAVENGER

The sky was darkening as Tom and
Elenna flew down among the trees,
and Storm's hooves touched down
on the scrubby grass beside the body
of Arcta. Tom slid off the saddle and
ran to the mountain giant. He pushed
his hands through Arcta's fur, but it
was as cold as ice. A few hairs were

ruffled by the evening breeze, but the Beast made no other movement.

Tom closed his eyes tightly, trying to contain his rage. *You'll pay for this, Malvel!* Then his eyes flicked open as he felt a warm pulsing at his belt. The red jewel embedded in it was softly glowing, its magic activated by the presence of a Beast. His heart leapt.

"What does it mean?" asked Elenna, frowning at the red glow.

"It means Arcta is alive," said Tom, laying a hand on the Beast's massive chest. "But only just. I can't feel a heartbeat." The Beast's eyes were shut too, and no breath passed his lips.

"It must be some kind of magical sleep," said Elenna thoughtfully. "Like with Epos and Aduro."

Tom clambered up on to the Beast's chest and drew his sword, waving it at the vultures circling above. "Get away! Go on, all of you!"

Storm reared up and let out a fearsome neigh, and the birds scattered, cawing angrily.

"Let's cover him with branches for now," said Elenna. "That will give him some protection."

Tom leaped down next to her, and used his sword to hack leafy branches from the fallen trees. Then together they spread them out over the fallen mountain giant. Arcta was far too big to be covered entirely, but at least with a blanket of greenery

he was mostly hidden from view.

Tom turned to gaze up at the peak
of the mountain. Peering through
the dusk, he could still make out the
dark stripe of the column's shadow,
leading up to the very summit.

"Let's go," he said. He went to stroke Storm's nose. "You stay here, boy. Look after Arcta till we're back."

They set off in silence, climbing side by side out of the woodland until Storm and Arcta were out of sight. The ground was steep, and they were soon panting as they hopped up from rock to rock, following the path of the shadow as it led them higher and higher, around the side of the mountain.

The sky grew darker all the time, and a pale moon shone down on them, glimmering off pools of ice-cold mountain water nestled here and there among the rocks. The shadow was still plain to see, somehow blacker than the night itself.

Then from up ahead, Tom heard a low voice chanting strange words.

Darting around an outcrop of rocks, he saw the mountainside fall away beyond. It sloped down to a large placid lake, silvered by the moonlight. And on a boulder jutting out above the lake stood a familiar figure in long green robes.

Tom felt a chill creep across his skin.

Malvel!

The wizard was facing away from them, gazing out over the lake, and in his hands...

"It's the *Book of Derthsin*!" hissed

Elenna, arriving at Tom's side.

Malvel was reading out loud from the heavy, leather-bound spell book, his voice dripping with evil. As he chanted, the wizard cast his left hand out, trailing purple smoke which formed twisting patterns in the air – ancient symbols which Tom had never seen before.

Whatever spell he's casting, we have to stop him!

"Are we close enough for your bow?" whispered Tom.

Elenna nodded and drew an arrow, fitting it to her bowstring. She closed one eye and took aim, the string creaking as she drew it back.

"Be careful," said Tom. "We only

need to wound him to stop the
magic."

Whhhshh!

The arrow whipped away into the night. But at the same instant, Malvel whirled around, his green robes flapping, and flung his hand out towards them. A bird's cry split the air, and Tom saw in astonishment that Elenna's arrow had been transformed into a crow. It circled and flew away, cawing in confusion.

Malvel shut the *Book of Derthsin* with a bang. Then he smiled at Tom, his eyes glittering triumphantly. "Now, now... Is that any way to treat an old friend? Especially when I've prepared such a nice surprise for you..."

The wizard held out the book, and Tom saw that purple smoke was rising from its pages now, coiling up into the darkness. The ground began to shake so much that Tom almost lost his footing.

With a thunderous roar, something huge burst from the ground between Tom and Malvel, shattering solid rock and scattering boulders that went bouncing down the mountain.

Tom watched in horror as a creature rose up and shook himself. It was a hulking Beast bent down on all fours like a dog. Looming over Tom and Elenna, he was more than twice their height and heavily muscled. His body was coated in spiky white fur, all except for his tail which coiled like a serpent's, smooth and scaled.

The Beast drew his green lips into
a snarl to reveal curving white fangs,
while his savage eyes flashed orange

like a furnace.

Another creature from the Netherworld...

"Behold Skrar the Night Scavenger," cried Malvel. "The last Beast you will ever face!"

BOILING FURY

Tom's heart was racing, but he drew
his sword and stepped out to face
the Beast. "Is this overgrown dog
all you've got, Malvel?" he asked.
"Hardly even a challenge."

Skrar's fur prickled, every hair
standing on end, and the next
moment his whole body burst into
purplish flames.

Tom stumbled backwards, blasted by heat. *I spoke too soon!* He summoned the power of Ferno's scale, set into his shield, but nothing

happened. *Of course!* The scale was just as grey and cold as the other tokens. It would not protect him from flame the way it had on many of Tom's previous Quests.

Skrar prowled forward, massive claws crunching rocks beneath them. His blazing fur lit the mountainside with a fierce purple glow. Tom felt sweat break out on his brow at the sheer heat, and took another step back. *It's like standing beside Uncle Henry's forge!*

Then all at once, the flames flickered and died away, leaving only the ghostly white fur as Skrar advanced through the darkness.

"He can't keep this up for very

long," hissed Elenna. "We'll have to strike before—"

Whoomph! The flames burst into life again. With every step, Skrar sent plumes of smoke trailing from his claws, as they melted the ground beneath.

Tom swallowed hard. *If those claws even touch me, I'm dead!*

Then Skrar pounced, his two front paws outstretched.

Tom dodged as the Beast landed, shaking the ground. Pivoting, Tom brought his sword whirling round at the Beast's jaws. *Thunk!* The blade lodged in one of Skrar's massive teeth, sending a judder down Tom's sword arm.

Skrar let out a rumbling growl, then jerked his head sideways. Tom felt his feet leave the ground as he clung on to the sword hilt, and the Beast threw him aside, dislodging the blade and sending Tom bouncing and rolling among the rocks until his

back struck a boulder so hard that his teeth rattled.

He sat there, his head swimming as he checked his body for any damage. *Just scrapes…* But before he could get up, Skrar was on him, claws scything down.

Tom launched himself to one side, and went tumbling down a steep slope. Sharp rocks scratched at him as he rolled over and over, until he grabbed a boulder and came sliding to a halt.

Tom rose groggily to his feet, feeling weak, with Malvel's laughter ringing in his ears. Up on the higher ground, he saw that Skrar's flames had died away again, and Elenna had an arrow fitted to her bowstring. *Thump! Thump! Thump!* Elenna unleashed arrow after arrow, each one hitting Skrar's hide like the beat of a drum.

The Beast growled in fury. Then – *whoomph!* The flames leapt up again, and Elenna's missiles fell away, instantly crumbling into ash.

"There has to be some way to get past those flames!" said Tom.

He glanced all around, and saw that he had fallen so far that he was only a short distance from the shore of the mountain lake. Perhaps if he could just get the Beast to enter the water, he could put out the fire. *And maybe Skrar's heavy fur will weigh him down!*

Tom cupped his hands and shouted up the mountainside. "Come and fight me, Skrar! Unless you fear the Master of the Beasts!" Bending down, he picked up the biggest rock he could find and hurled it with all his strength. The rock bounced off the Beast's flank, and Skrar turned his massive head to glare at him.

"I don't know what you think you're doing, Tom, but it won't work!" snarled Malvel.

Tom ignored the wizard, picked up a second rock and threw it at Skrar.

Rrroaarr! With a fearsome growl, Skrar flicked his great tail and launched himself down the mountainside. His massive paws ate

up the distance between them.

Tom turned and ran, hurtling full tilt down the mountainside. His boots splashed into the icy cold shallows, and water flooded them in an instant. He plunged onwards, wading as fast as he could into the lake. Behind him, he heard a mighty crash of spray as Skrar followed him.

It's now or never...

Drawing a deep breath, Tom dived beneath the surface.

BURIED

Tom kicked his legs, powering through the freezing water. Beneath him he could see the bed of the lake, a rocky surface only dimly visible through the murk. There was no sound but a muffled roar that filled his ears.

Where's the Beast?

Turning his head, Tom felt his

heart lurch. A vast white bulk was silently looming towards him. Skrar's fur streamed back, jaws opening wide. Any moment now, those teeth would come clamping down on Tom's feet...

Tom twisted sideways, just as the jaws swung shut in a flurry of bubbles. He spun round and clamped the Beast's snout shut, pulling it towards him so that Skrar couldn't open his mouth.

The Beast thrashed Tom from side to side, but Tom drew on the power of the golden breastplate. Magical strength flooded through his limbs, just enough to let him cling on.

Whhuummmph! Skrar shot

upwards and broke the surface, lifting Tom with him. Tom blinked away water and sucked in a deep breath. He caught a glimpse of the darkened sky above, then they were plunging down again, diving beneath the surface.

Even with the magic of the breastplate, Tom's arm muscles burned as he strained to hold Skrar's jaws shut. Then all at once, the Beast relaxed. They sank deeper and deeper, the lake darkening. Tom felt the water getting hotter, as though they were sinking through a warm bath.

It must be Skrar. He's heating the lake with the magic of his fur...

The water grew hotter still. It was almost boiling, and Tom couldn't stand it any more. With one powerful kick he darted towards the shallows.

The water was bubbling as he stumbled up into the open air. Elenna was waiting anxiously on the bank, and when she saw him she waded in, grabbing him by the collar and yanking him the last few steps. They collapsed together on the ground. Tom's skin pulsed with the heat, and his clothes were steaming.

"Look!" gasped Elenna, pointing at the lake.

Steam was rising all across the surface now, and the water frothed furiously. Tom watched in

astonishment as the lake began to shrink, receding on every side. *It's evaporating!*

In just a few moments the whole lake had billowed up into the sky as steam, and as it cleared Tom

saw the wide, bare rocky basin left
behind. In the centre crouched the
Beast, curled up in a ball, his fur
flattened against his body.

"Skrar's not moving," said
Elenna, frowning. "I think using

all that magic must have weakened him."

"Now's our chance!" said Tom.

Gripping his sword hilt tightly, he clambered down into the empty lake bed. "Give up, Skrar!" he called, striding towards the Beast. "If you surrender, I won't hurt you."

But still Skrar didn't move. Tom slowed as he got closer, holding his shield up high in case the Beast lashed out.

A noise like a thunderclap rang out from above, and the ground shuddered.

Turning, Tom saw the distant figure of Malvel further up the mountainside. The Dark Wizard

flung out his hands and a bolt of
purple magic streaked from his
fingers into the rock below him
with a second thunderous impact.
The ground shook again, but this
time some rocks broke off and went
bouncing down towards the lake.
Tom lost his footing and stumbled.

"He's trying to start an

avalanche!" yelled Elenna. "Careful, Tom – he'll kill you and the Beast if he has to!"

A third bolt shot from Malvel's outstretched hands. *CRRRASSH!* The mountainside collapsed and a wave of rocks came hammering down into the empty lake.

A boulder slammed into Tom's

shins, knocking his legs out from under him. Sprawled on the ground, he swung his shield up over his head, and felt it jolt as another rock struck it. *We're going to be buried alive!* He cast a glance back, and saw that the motionless form of Skrar was already half covered by falling rocks.

"Hold on!" shouted Elenna.

Peering round the edge of his shield, Tom saw that she was fitting an arrow to her bowstring. In one swift movement she had loosed it, and it flew straight at Malvel's head...

But with a twitch of his cloak, the wizard vanished. *He's escaped us again!* Tom gritted his teeth and rose, lowering his shield. Digging deep, he drew on the power of the golden boots. Magical strength surged through his legs and he leapt up high, trying to escape the avalanche.

"Tom, no!" yelled Elenna.

For an instant, Tom saw a grey mass looming through the air towards him, a wall of solid rock. Then there was an explosion of pain, and everything went black.

6

NEW ENEMIES

"Tom? Wake up, Tom!"

Someone was leaning over him. He blinked, and Elenna's face blurred into view, pale against the night sky. "You got knocked out," she said.

Tom's head felt like someone was attacking it with a battering ram. "What happened?" he murmured.

"A rock hit you in mid-air," Elenna explained. "A big one. If you ask me, you're lucky to be alive."

Tom's lips curled into a grin. Then it all came flooding back – Malvel, the lake, the fight with Skrar... He propped himself up on his elbows, and saw that he was still lying in the empty lake. The avalanche was over, and silence reigned. "Where's the Beast?" he asked.

Elenna pointed. Turning his head, Tom saw that the rocks had all come to rest in the centre of the lake, heaped up in a giant mound. "Malvel buried him alive," said Elenna.

Sure enough, Tom could just see

a glimpse of white fur among the rubble. *So Skrar has been defeated...* But he didn't feel any joy in the victory. Something didn't feel right.

"There's no golden column this time," said Tom.

"Maybe that was only for Grymon," said Elenna, but she didn't sound very sure. "So there's no shadow for us to follow... What now?"

Tom rose to his feet, wincing. His head swam, and he had to steady himself with his sword. "Only one thing we can do – go after Malvel."

"He disappeared into thin air, remember?" said Elenna. "He could be anywhere by now."

Just then, a panicked whinny echoed out across the mountainside. Tom and Elenna looked up together. There, circling overhead, was the dark shape of Storm, his raven's wings almost invisible against the black sky. He swooped down and landed next to them with a great gust of air. He whinnied again, and stamped a front hoof.

An uneasy feeling stirred in Tom's heart. "What's wrong, Storm?" he asked. "Why have you left Arcta?"

"Let's go with him," Elenna suggested.

Tom nodded, and they climbed up on to Storm's back. At once the stallion leapt into the air, wings beating as he carried them away from the dry lake bed.

They curved round the side of the mountain, with no light to guide them but a shining moon and the first glimmering of the stars. "Isn't that the woodland where Arcta fell?" said Elenna suddenly.

Tom looked, and felt his throat dry up. There was the patch of crushed trees where the mountain giant had fallen. But Arcta himself was nowhere to be seen.

He scanned around and saw other trees had been cut down, creating a pathway from Arcta's resting place. "Someone must have taken him away," said Tom.

"A whole crowd of people, more like," said Elenna. "And they must have driven Storm off too. But where have they gone?"

"I think I know," said Tom, grimly.

He had caught sight of something in the distance, away from the mountains. A glimmer of fire on the horizon, back the way they had come. "It's Ched's village," he said. He flicked the reins, and Storm veered away, soaring out over the countryside towards the village.

"Use the golden helmet," said Elenna. "What can you see?"

As he drew on the power of the helmet, Tom felt his vision sharpen with magic. Gazing at the village, he saw people in the marketplace all crowding around Arcta's body with flaming torches. Ropes had been tied around the mountain giant's limbs, and the strongest of

the villagers were heaving at them, straining to drag the Beast into position on top of a large mound of wood...

Tom gasped as he realised.

"They're building him a funeral pyre. They want to burn his body!"

Elenna clutched his waist a little tighter. "But he's not dead yet," she muttered.

Storm beat his wings faster, as though sensing the urgency in their voices. They began to dive, the wind rushing through Tom's hair and making his eyes water as they came speeding down over the rooftops.

Tom didn't need his helmet to see a man climbing a ladder propped up by the pyre, holding a flaming torch. *It's Ched! And he's about to burn Arcta alive...*

Elenna's hands let go of Tom's waist, and a moment later an arrow zipped past his ear. *Whhhhhsssshh!*

Ched cried out in shock as the torch fell to the ground, with Elenna's shaft stuck through it.

Thump! Storm landed on all four hooves in front of the pyre, jolting Tom and Elenna in the saddle. Tom vaulted to the ground, drawing his sword.

The nearest villagers whirled round. They watched, their eyes glittering with suspicion in the light of the torches, as Elenna climbed down beside Tom.

"What are you doing here?" Ched demanded, still halfway up the ladder. There was no trace of friendliness in his voice.

"You can't do this," Tom told him. "Don't you see? Arcta's not dead!"

Ched snorted nastily. "He looks dead to me."

Out of the corner of his eye, Tom noticed that the crowd was pressing closer around him and Elenna. Some of them had weapons as well as torches – rusted old billhooks, daggers and even a frying pan clutched by a frail old woman.

"We have many customs in our village," said Ched. "But the most important of all is that the dead are burned. They must be, or else they will come back as evil spirits to haunt us!"

"That's nonsense!" snapped Elenna.

A hostile murmur ran among the crowd, and Ched's face reddened with anger. "Is it, now?" he snarled. "Then what of the Dark Wizard? Hasn't Malvel returned from the dead to plague us once again? If you had burned his body, as we do here, it would never have happened. It's your fault, Tom! Just because they call you Master of the Beasts, that doesn't mean you're always right. We will honour Arcta as he deserves... with fire!"

As Ched spoke, Tom could have sworn something glimmered in his eyes. *Was that a flash of green? Could Malvel be behind all this?* But his thoughts were interrupted by the

sight of a villager handing a freshly
lit torch up to Ched.

"I'm warning you for the last

time," said Tom. He crouched down, lifting his shield and sword. "I don't want to fight you, but I will if I must."

Angry voices rose from the crowd, and they pressed in closer still, their makeshift weapons gleaming. Tom gripped his sword hilt tightly, but he couldn't bring himself to attack. Most of the villagers looked old enough to be his grandparents. Some of them were children, hardly out of swaddling clothes.

"What do we do?" whispered Elenna. Her back was pressed up against his, as they faced the circle of villagers. Tom glanced over his shoulder and saw she had an arrow ready on her bowstring.

"I don't know," he said. "But we can't hurt them."

Elenna nodded. "Agreed."

An old man rushed forward and seized Tom's sword hand. *If I throw him off, I'll probably break his arm!* Reluctantly, Tom let the man take his weapon. Someone else snatched his shield, while others seized his limbs and held him in place. A man in a blacksmith's apron wound a thick rope around Tom's arms and body and tied it securely. From the sound of it, Tom guessed that Elenna was being tied up too.

"Well done, all of you!" cried Ched. "You have protected our village. Now these traitors must pay for their crimes – for letting the earthquake wreck our homes, and for trying to stop us from burning the mountain giant." He raised his hand and pointed to the heap of wood. "There is only one worthy punishment... Throw them both on the pyre!"

DEATH BY FIRE

"You're all crazy!" yelled Elenna, as the villagers shoved her and Tom, stumbling, towards the pyre. Tom strained his muscles, trying to worm his way out of the ropes, but they held firm. *Maybe it was a mistake to let them disarm us after all...*

The villagers bundled Tom and Elenna over to two enormous men standing on a platform by the pyre. The two men took Elenna first, swinging her by her shoulders and feet, then tossing her up on top of the pyre like a sack of grain being loaded on to a cart. Next they took Tom, and flung him up beside her.

Oof! Tom landed awkwardly on the pile of wood, one arm crushed against his side. He rolled over on to his back. Arcta lay beside him, a mountain of brown fur, and Elenna was groaning a short distance away. The sharp smell of oil filled his nostrils. *They must have soaked the kindling with it so that it will catch fire more quickly.*

Turning his head, Tom saw the

figure of Ched still standing on the ladder, silhouetted against the night sky. He held his flaming torch aloft. Any moment now, he would light the pyre.

"This isn't you, Ched," said Tom, his voice hoarse. "You're not thinking straight. The Ched I know would never hurt an innocent Beast. It's Malvel – he must have bewitched you. If you'll just untie me, I can—"

"Silence!" roared Ched. Then his arm came down in an arc, the torch trailing flames as it struck the pyre. At once, the wood began to snap and crackle, and the smell of smoke filled the night air. A ragged cheer rose up from the crowd as Ched leapt from the ladder, landing in a crouch on the ground.

Tom flexed his muscles again, but the ropes were strong and well tied. "Elenna!" he shouted. "Can you get free?"

Elenna grunted with effort, then called back. "No chance, Tom."

A wave of heat washed across the top of the pyre. Beyond the body of Arcta, Tom could see the flames licking up, belching out smoke which drifted towards them and clouded his view. He inhaled fumes, and coughed. *Not long to come up with a plan.*

Then Tom caught a glimpse of something through the smoke, way above. A pale bird flying through the black sky. *No, not a bird... It's Storm! He must have flown off while the villagers were tying us up.*

Pursing his lips, Tom let out a shrill whistle. The stallion swooped lower at the sound, curving round towards the marketplace. As Storm soared closer, Tom shouted as loud as he could. "The pyre! Smash the pyre!"

Villagers surged through the marketplace to meet Storm, waving their torches at him. But as the stallion spread his wings and swooped down, they cowered away. Storm landed by the giant heap of wood, folding his wings. He reared up, both forelegs flailing. One brave man made a lunge for the reins, but Storm jolted forward, barging the man aside and knocking him to the ground.

Storm snorted, lowering his head

as he charged straight at the base of
the pyre.

Thunk! Storm drove his hooves
hard into a wooden support
somewhere below, and Tom felt the
whole pyre judder.

"That's it, boy!" shouted Elenna.

Thunk! Storm kicked again, and this time the pyre groaned as it sagged slowly to one side.

"Someone stop that horse!" yelled Ched.

THUNK! At the third impact, Tom felt the wood give way beneath him. There was a thunderous crash. Then a shower of sparks leapt up as the pyre sank under its own weight, tilting at an angle. Tom went rolling, over and over. He heard Elenna cry out in shock. He caught a glimpse of Ched's face twisted in a snarl of fury. He saw Arcta sliding across the wood, then felt a *THUD* like an earthquake as the Beast struck the ground. Then

Tom himself landed with a bump, rolling to a halt at last against the heavy wheel of a cart.

Shouts of panic rose up all around. A short distance away, Tom saw a torch which lay abandoned, still burning. Squirming his way over to it, he held his ropes against the flame until they caught. At once the fire spread to the sleeve of his tunic. The heat of it singed his skin and made him gasp with pain. *Need to weaken the rope... Just...enough...*

Tom channelled all his strength into his arms, as he forced them steadily away from his body. The ropes held for a moment, then snapped, leaving two blackened, burning ends.

Quickly, Tom shrugged off the rope and rolled on the ground, snuffing out the flames on his tunic. Then he sat up, scanning the marketplace.

Elenna lay nearby, sawing at her own ropes with a dagger she must have picked up from the ground. Beyond her, villagers ran every which way, some bringing buckets of water to hurl at the blazing pyre. It made no difference – the fire raged fiercer than ever, with the massive form of Arcta lying sprawled beside it.

"What are you doing?" roared Ched, striding into view from behind the pyre. "Drag the Beast on to the flames! Burn him to ashes!"

Not if I can help it!

Tom went to draw his sword, then remembered it was gone. Instead he snatched up the torch and sped off, racing around the edge of the pyre so that he came up behind Ched. *Just a few more steps!* But at the last moment, Ched whirled round and aimed a savage kick at Tom's stomach. Dodging, Tom flailed with the torch, forcing Ched to stumble away.

"No!" shouted Tom. But it was too late. Ched lost his footing and fell headlong into the pyre.

Ched curled into a ball, hissing like a snake as the flames took hold. Then Tom realised with a jolt

that it wasn't Ched hissing at all. A
strange, ghostly form was swirling
up from the villager's body, barely
visible among the fumes of smoke.
Tom would have known that figure
anywhere.

Malvel!

The spectre seemed to glare at Tom for an instant, its eyes flashing green. Then it was gone, curling away into the sky. *So Ched was under a spell, after all...*

Tom dropped his torch and darted forward. Grabbing Ched under his arms, he pulled the villager back from the fire. "Help!" he yelled, and two villagers ran in with buckets. They emptied them on to Ched, dousing the flames at once.

Coughing and spluttering, Ched sat up, soaking wet. Tom met his eyes, and his heart flooded with relief. He could see at once that his old friend was back to normal.

"Where am I?" asked Ched. "I don't... I don't remember anything."

"Sorcery!" screeched a young woman nearby. "Some horrible ghost possessed our leader!"

"We can talk about that later!" shouted Elenna. Tom saw his friend approaching, carrying a bucket of water in each hand. "Right now we need to save Arcta. Who's with me?"

The Beast's fur was finally ablaze, smoke billowing up from it. But in just a few moments Elenna had rallied the villagers to pour their buckets on to the burning mountain giant. The flames hissed as they were doused, and yet more smoke drifted up into the night sky. When the last of the fire had been put out, Arcta lay as still as ever. His fur hung off in patches, blackened and scorched. *Have we done enough to save him?*

"Tom," croaked Ched. "I did this, didn't I? I'm so sorry."

"It wasn't your fault," Tom told him. "And you're safe now. We all are."

The words had barely left his mouth when a blood-curdling shriek rang out over the village. It seemed to linger in the air, and for an instant Tom felt as though an icy hand had gripped his heart.

He gazed towards the dark peaks of the Northern Mountains. Even without the power of the golden helmet, he could see something approaching from that direction – a hulking white Beast, racing across the rocky landscape. It was already

halfway to the village. It seemed impossible, but there was only one explanation.

Skrar is back from the dead!

RESURRECTED

As Tom watched, Skrar's body
lit up with a burst of flame. The
Beast charged onwards, a fireball
barrelling towards the village. *And
it won't be long before he gets here!*

"I don't understand," said Elenna.
"I thought Skrar had been buried
alive!"

"He must have dug himself out,"

said Tom, grimly.

"What do we do?" asked Ched.

Tom looked around at the terrified faces of the villagers. They were all watching him now, expecting him to save them from the Beast. *But how?* If Skrar could survive a mountain avalanche like that, what could Tom possibly do to defeat him?

"Everyone stay calm," said Tom.

A horrified murmur ran amongst the crowd, and Tom saw that Skrar was racing through a forest now, not far from the village. Every tree he passed caught fire, sending gouts of black smoke trailing into the night sky. He burst into the open, careering like a runaway cart. Tom

saw the Beast's jaws gaping wide,
his eyes blazing orange.

"Save us!" wailed an old man.
"Please, Master of the Beasts!"

*There has to be some way to stop
Skrar!*

Tom glanced all around, his gaze
falling on a pile of tree trunks at
the side of the marketplace, with
the branches cut off. *Of course – the
villagers must have rolled Arcta
here on those trunks.* And suddenly
he had an idea.

"Listen, I know how to stop
Skrar!" he shouted. He leapt up
on to the smouldering remains of
the pyre. "But I need all of you.
Together, we have a chance, if you're

ready to stand and fight."

One by one, the villagers began to nod.

"We'll defend our village to our dying breaths," said Ched. "We're with you."

Tom grinned. "Then get the biggest tree trunk you can carry and come with me. And bring some ropes, too."

"I'll keep Skrar busy!" said Elenna.

As Elenna leapt up into Storm's saddle and took off, Tom strode down the main dusty road, leading the crowd to the edge of the village. He could hear the thunder of the Beast's paws now, as Skrar bore down on them, still blazing with fire.

Tom noticed the villagers casting anxious glances at the approaching Beast. "Don't be afraid," he told them. "Just concentrate on the tree trunk. Tie the ropes to the end of it and hoist it up beside the road."

The villagers got to work, and in a few moments they were heaving on the ropes. Gradually the trunk rose until it stood, teetering on its end. "Now hold it steady," Tom commanded. "Until I give the word. Then you let go."

Elenna swooped above them on Storm, an arrow ready on her bowstring. "Make sure Skrar stays on the road!" Tom shouted up at her. Elenna nodded. Then she loosed her first arrow, sending it zipping through the night. Skrar let out a savage roar as the missile lodged in his side.

Some of the villagers shrank back in

terror, and Tom smiled to reassure them. But fear was stirring in his own heart. *We'll only get one chance to bring the Beast down. Can I rely on these people?*

Elenna fired a second arrow, and Skrar gave another feral cry. But as the Beast approached the village, he slowed down. He prowled forward, then came to a halt at last, planting his paws firmly on the road. He was so close that Tom could feel the heat coming off his fur. Arching his back, Skrar glared at Tom, drool dripping from his jaws. *It's like he knows he's walking into a trap... But I've got to convince him to do it anyway!*

Tom took a deep breath and

stepped out into the road, approaching the Beast. He felt helpless without his sword and shield, but he made himself keep walking.

Skrar's fur was torn and bleeding all across his body from the blows of the boulders. The Beast's legs shuddered, as though he barely had the strength to stand. But Tom knew that those vicious claws could still rip him apart in an instant.

Drawing on the power of the red jewel, Tom spoke to the Beast inside his mind. *What's wrong, Skrar? Are you afraid?*

Skrar's voice answered him, a low growl that sent a shiver through

Tom's body. *I fear nothing, Master of the Beasts. I am a creature of the Netherworld, and I will tear you limb from limb!*

Tom forced out a laugh. *If you say so. To me, you seem as weak as a newborn puppy!*

Skrar snarled. Then he lunged forward, ears flattened, teeth glinting.

Tom turned and ran, his heart pounding. He pumped his legs, racing as fast as he could towards the village. The ground rumbled as Skrar bounded after him, his massive paws shaking the road with every impact.

"Now!" Tom yelled, as he raced

past the mass of villagers holding
up the trunk. He dived forward,
twisting as he fell. He saw the Beast
charging, trailing fire, and the
villagers letting go of their ropes.
The trunk tilted, slowly at first, then
faster, coming down like an axe on a

butcher's block.

THUMP! The trunk smashed into Skrar's back, driving the Beast down on to the road. Skrar's eyes widened with fury as he collapsed, trapped under the weight of the trunk. He squirmed, claws flailing,

and the villagers shoved at each other to get clear. But the night scavenger was firmly pinned down. All across his fur, the flames began to die out, until Skrar was nothing more than a hulking white dog, lying defeated on the road.

Tom got to his feet, shaking. He looked around and spotted the old man who had taken his weapons, goggling in amazement at the fallen Beast. Tom gently took his shield and sword out of the man's hands, then strode towards Skrar. The Beast watched him with fury, but though he strained his muscles, he couldn't get free.

Smoke prickled at Tom's nostrils

and stung his eyes as he bent down and laid the flat of his blade against Skrar's neck. "It's over," he said gently. "Will you surrender now?"

Skrar didn't reply. Then his whole body burst into bright flame one more time, making Tom stumble backwards. A great gasp rose up from the villagers.

The Beast's body seemed to be disintegrating, the white fur fading into thick smoke that swirled up around the trunk. There was a heavy thud as the trunk rose up, flipping and landing on the road a short distance away, and the last of Skrar went drifting up into the sky.

"Is it gone?" asked Ched.

As if in reply, the air shimmered above where the Beast had lain, and a tall golden column took shape, glittering in the darkness. At the top of it was the sculpted face of a giant dog. *Skrar!* And from the base of the column, a dark line of shadow

stretched away through the trees, leading south.

Tom realised he had been holding his breath, and let it out in a sigh. "Yes," he said wearily. "It's gone."

Storm came gliding down to land at Tom's side, and Elenna swung herself out of the saddle. She clapped Tom on the back, grinning. "We did it!"

Tom nodded. "We all did." He turned to the villagers. "Your home is safe now, thanks to your courage!"

"And yours, Tom and Elenna," said Ched. "Three cheers for the Master of the Beasts!"

Tom smiled as the villagers clustered around them, laughing, cheering and chattering excitedly to one another. But all the same, he couldn't help feeling uneasy. Above the crowd he could see the last wisps of smoke rising up from the scorched body of Arcta. The mountain giant was still stricken by Malvel's sorcery. *And no doubt the other Good Beasts of Avantia have suffered the same fate.*

Whilst Malvel was still free, there was no time to celebrate.

THE END

CONGRATULATIONS,
YOU HAVE COMPLETED THIS QUEST!

At the end of each chapter you were awarded a special gold coin.
The QUEST in this book was worth an amazing 8 coins.

Look at the Beast Quest totem picture inside the back cover of this book to see how far you've come in your journey to become

MASTER OF THE BEASTS.

The more books you read, the more coins you will collect!

Do you want your own
Beast Quest Totem?

1. Cut out and collect the coin below
2. Go to the Beast Quest website
3. Download and print out your totem
4. Add your coin to the totem
www.beastquest.co.uk/totem

Don't miss the next exciting Beast Quest book, TARANTIX THE BONE SPIDER!

Read on for a sneak peek...

THE UNNATURAL STORM

Tom leaned low over Storm's back, his eyes narrowed against the howling wind and driving rain. Elenna, in the saddle behind Tom, clung tightly to his waist. Storm's huge, feathered wings beat hard, carrying them swiftly through the night. Tom felt a rush of gratitude towards Lyra, the young witch from Henkrall who had given Storm the magical wings. Without her help, the journey would have been almost impossible.

Dark, tattered clouds streamed past as they flew, and above the roar of the wind in his ears, Tom could hear the crash and boom of waves far below. The first blood-red glimmer of dawn streaked the eastern sky, and looking down, Tom could just make out the slender line of shadow they were following, cast on to the raging ocean. He and Elenna had already defeated two Beasts, summoned by Malvel from the Netherworld using the stolen *Book of Derthsin*. After each victory, a magical totem had sprung up from the ground, casting a long shadow directing them towards the next stage of their Quest. This time, the totem's shadow led south. And if the last two Beasts were anything to go by, Tom knew Malvel would have summoned something truly evil to face them.

Gusts of wind tore at Tom's hair and clothes as Storm swooped over heaving waves that pounded in a wild fury against the shoreline.

"Someone's in trouble!" Elenna cried, pointing. Through the towering

cascades of spray thrown up by
the huge breakers, Tom could see
a jumble of huts on the shore.

Scurrying figures dragged fishing boats up the beach, away from the crashing waves. The smashed remains of several boats already churned in the shallows.

"Without Sepron to calm the waters, the villagers are at the mercy of the storm," Elenna shouted over the wind.

Tom glanced at his shield. All the magical tokens there, including Sepron the Sea Serpent's green scale, had faded to a dull grey. Malvel had cast a spell, sending the wizard Aduro and all the Good Beasts into a death-like sleep. Until Daltec and Lyra found an antidote to the spell, Tom could no longer call on the

Beasts for aid.

Tom's chest tightened at the thought of delaying their Quest, but he had no choice. "We have to help them," he said. As Storm swooped lower, Tom kept his eyes on a knot of struggling villagers. A flash of lightning bleached his vision. Thunder boomed right overhead, making Tom tense up, half expecting to be hit.

"Rafe!" An anguished cry pierced though the thunder's echoing rumble. "Rafe!"

A tall woman stood among the breaking waves, her long hair and sodden clothes whipping about her as two broad men tried to pull her towards the shore. The pain in the woman's eyes as she gazed out to the churning ocean made Tom's pulse quicken. *Someone's lost at sea!*

Storm landed on the beach at a canter, kicking up wet sand, then pulled to a stop. Tom and Elenna swung from the saddle and waded into the crashing waves. Icy water sucked at Tom's legs, tugging and slapping all round him. The struggling woman sobbed breathlessly, fighting against the two men that held her.

Read
TARANTIX THE BONE SPIDER
to find out what happens next!

Fight the Beasts,
Fear the Magic

Do you want to know more
about BEAST QUEST?
Then join our Quest Club!

Visit
www.beastquest.co.uk/club
and sign up today!

Are you a collector of the Beast Quest Cards?
Visit the website for further information.

AVAILABLE SPRING 2018

The epic adventure is brought to life on **Xbox One** and **PS4** for the first time ever!

www.maximumgames.com   www.beast-quest.com